NAUGHTY NELLO

NELLO

AND

THE SAUSAGES

NAUGHTY NELLO AND THE SAUSAGES

by

Joanne Puccinelli

RoseDog🐾Books
PITTSBURGH, PENNSYLVANIA 15222

The contents of this work including, but not limited to, the accuracy of events, people, and places depicted; opinions expressed; permission to use previously published materials included; and any advice given or actions advocated are solely the responsibility of the author, who assumes all liability for said work and indemnifies the publisher against any claims stemming from publication of the work.

ISBN: 978-1-4349-8049-6
eISBN: 978-1-4349-4290-6
Printed in the United States of America

First Printing

For more information or to order additional books, please contact:
RoseDog Books
701 Smithfield Street
Pittsburgh, Pennsylvania 15222
U.S.A.
1-800-834-1803
www.rosedogbookstore.com

SUMMARY OF THE BOOK

Meet **Naughty Nello** in the first of his many escapades. **Nello** is a curious boy. He lives with his parents, sisters, and brothers in a poor neighborhood rich in different ethnic cultures. His parents are from the "Old Country" and have kept some of their old ways in America. His first adventure, **Naughty Nello and the Sausages**, helps him learn that not everything old is bad and not everything new is better. In this hilarious story, **Nello** lands in a heap of trouble trying to answer questions about his heritage. However, despite the turmoil he creates, **Naughty Nello** gains a new respect for the "old ways" and his family.

Naughty Nello and the Sausages is a story not only children love, but it is a story for adults who want to instill respect for diversity in the young. **Naughty Nello** learns the importance of honesty and family. It is a story of disappointment and forgiveness. Although the story takes place in another era, the lessons learned by **Naughty Nello** are relevant to life in America today.—life in this great "Melting Pot."

Dedicated to

Nello & Inez Puccinelli

and their descendents

NAUGHTY NELLO AND THE SAUSAGES

by Joanne Puccinelli

Naughty Nello lived with his Papa, Mama, two brothers, and two sisters in a big white house right in the middle of the block.

Papa and Mama had lived in this house for a long time—ever since they had crossed the great big ocean to come from Italy to the New Country so that Papa could work at the smelter in Anaconda.

Papa and Mama still talked about the Old Country and sometimes Naughty Nello could hear longing and sadness in their voices. This is what he couldn't understand. Wouldn't anyone rather have a New Country than an Old Country?

When Naughty Nello asked Papa about this, Papa just smiled and said, "Someday when you are big, you will understand."

Then Papa continued to smoke his pipe.

Mama had answered by telling Naughty Nello how her family, his ancestors, had lived in Italy for hundreds of years and that is what made Italy the Old Country. This helped him understand a little bit better, but mainly it made him draw pictures in his mind of all his old ancestors. He planned some day to visit the Old Country and see for himself what was so wonderful about it. It was a strange thought to Naughty Nello that being old could be so special.

Naughty Nello could spend a lot of time thinking about the Old Country if it were not for all the other things that seemed strange and made Naughty Nello curious. Naughty Nello was not REALLY a naughty little boy, but he WAS a very curious boy.

It always amazed Naughty Nello when his curiosity got him into trouble. He truly wanted to be a good boy, and most of the time he was, but every once in awhile he'd become SO curious. He would act without thinking. Then Papa, Mama, and his two brothers and two sisters would get upset, and ask, "Why are you so naughty?"

This question really made Naughty Nello unhappy. He wanted to please his family. He loved his Papa, Mama, two brothers, and two sisters, but somehow there were just too many things he had to know, and this needing to know led to trouble. For example, there was the trouble with the **sausages**.

Papa and Mama took good care of their home and children. Some people might think they were poor, but their home was warm and Mama was an excellent cook. In fact, Naughty Nello believed his Mama was the best cook in this New World. He wasn't sure about the Old World though because Mama claimed she had learned to cook by helping her own Mama and Nonna (grandmother). So Naughty Nello believed The Old Country had many good cooks.

Of course, Papa helped with the meals by making a lot of their food. Papa would buy a pig and make headcheese, ham, salt pork, and wonderful sausages. Naughty Nello loved to watch Papa make all the food, but the making of the sausages especially fascinated him.

The day Naughty Nello got in trouble was the day Papa was making sausages. First, Papa ground the meat and added the special seasonings. Naughty Nello enjoyed watching all of this, but the best part was stuffing the casings. Papa explained to Naughty Nello that the casings were really the intestines of the pig. Naughty Nello watched Papa stuff the casings and then tie off sections. Finally, Papa hung the sausages from the ceiling in the pantry. Naughty Nello thought it was very odd to see sausages dangling above him.

Papa said the sausages must cure for a certain number of days before they would be ready to eat. When Papa had said they must cure, Naughty Nello asked if the sausages were sick. Papa laughed and explained that cured meant to age so the seasonings would blend and flavor the meat. This explanation helped a little, but not much.

As Naughty Nello saw the sausages hanging from the ceiling, he began wondering what the difference was between the New Sausages and the Old Sausages (the sausages which had been taken down from the ceiling after a long time of hanging in the pantry).

That night when Naughty Nello was in bed, he began thinking of all those New Sausages hanging from the ceiling in the pantry. He wondered if Papa might be wrong and that the New Sausages might just taste better than the Old Sausages. After all, Naughty Nello knew most things he liked were better new. He would much rather have new toys or clothes than old ones. And he certainly knew his little brothers, six-year old James and four-year old Frankie, would rather have new knickers than wear his old clothes.

Naughty Nello was seven years old and growing like a weed, at least that was what all the grownups remarked to his parents when they came visiting. He was glad he was the oldest because even though most of his clothes Mama made from Papa's worn out coveralls, every once in a while, he would get a new shirt or new pants. They were always so much better than the old ones, so certainly the New Sausages must be wonderful.

The more Naughty Nello thought about the sausages hanging in the pantry, the more curious he became as to whether he was right or wrong. Naughty Nello glanced at James and Frankie who were sound asleep in the bed next to him. His older sisters, Nellie and Delia, were also sleeping.

Naughty Nello decided he would go to the pantry and look at the sausages to see if they were being "cured". He knew he could make his way easily in the dark to the pantry. Then he would quietly close the pantry door and watch the sausages. Papa and Mama would never hear him.

So that is exactly what Naughty Nello did. The floorboards were cold as he lowered himself off the bed and made his way quietly and carefully out the back bedroom and into the kitchen. Once he heard James moan, and Naughty Nello had to stand very still until he was sure James was again sound asleep. As he passed through the kitchen, he could hear Papa's loud snoring coming from the front bedroom. It was only a few more steps to the pantry.

After entering the pantry, Naughty Nello carefully closed the door. It squeaked a little, and Naughty Nello's heart raced for a minute thinking Papa might wake and see him, but Papa was still snoring. Naughty Nello reached for the light cord, gave it a pull, and stood in the midst of hanging sausages.

They didn't really look much different then they did when Papa first hung them. Naughty Nello thought they looked a wee bit darker, but in his heart he knew New Sausages must taste better than Old Sausages. Was he right?? He had to know, so Naughty Nello decided he would take down one sausage and taste it for himself.

Naughty Nello spotted the very sausage he felt would taste the best. In order to reach it, he would have to stand on something. Naughty Nello spotted the flour barrel and knew if he could stand on it, he would be able to reach the sausage. Carefully, Naughty Nello pushed and pushed until the flour barrel was right under the rope of sausages hanging from the ceiling.

Naughty Nello climbed on top of the flour barrel. The top of the barrel did not seem too sturdy, but Naughty Nello knew it would support him. He lifted his arms and grabbed a rope of sausage. Just as he was about to give a big tug, the barrel lid collapsed! Naughty Nello gave a scream as he fell into the flour dragging the sausages with him.

He heard Mama scream. Then his two brothers and two sisters were screaming too. He heard heavy footsteps. Naughty Nello tried to wipe the flour out of his eyes. He heard Papa mutter something in the Old Country language and saw his HUGE Papa standing in the doorway. His Papa looked very angry. Naughty Nello looked around and saw flour and sausages everywhere in the pantry. Mama just stood in the doorway staring at him. Finally, she asked, "Nello, what have you done?"

Naughty Nello tried to explain about the New Sausages being better than the Old Sausages, but Papa and Mama just shook their heads. "Look at the mess! You will help clean!" growled Papa.

It took Papa, Mama, and Naughty Nello a long time to clean the pantry. Flour was everywhere. Papa had to restring all the sausages and hang them from the ceiling. Naughty Nello was very tired by the time he went to bed. He knew Papa and Mama must be very tired too. This made Naughty Nello feel badly because his Papa and Mama worked hard. Once again, he had been naughty.

He would help Mama all day in the kitchen and be extra good for Papa. Finally, Naughty Nello fell asleep resolving to be the very best boy anyone would want.

Naughty Nello slept for a long time. When he did awake, he sniffed the wonderful smell of sausage cooking. He jumped out of bed and ran into the kitchen. There were his Papa, Mama, two brothers, and two sisters. They were all grinning at him. Papa said, "Sit down, Nello. We have cooked some sausage. Most of the sausage is the Old Sausage, but there is one New Sausage for you to taste. You can see for yourself that the Old Sausage is better."

Naughty Nello gulped. " You are not mad at me?" he asked.

"Last night we were really mad at you, Nello, but today all we can do is laugh when we think of you in the flour barrel holding the sausages. We know you did not mean to do anything naughty, but next time you are curious, you must use good judgment and talk to Papa and Mama. Now, here is your breakfast. You have two sausages. The one on the right is the "cured" sausage and the other one is the New Sausage. Decide for yourself which tastes better."

Naughty Nello took a bite of the Old Sausage. It was the familiar spicy taste he loved. He took a bite of the New Sausage. Mmmmm! It was okay, but something was not as he thought. It did not have the flavor the Old Sausage had. Naughty Nello was tempted to tell his family the New Sausage tasted best, but that would be a lie, and had he not promised to be a very good boy?

Naughty Nello looked at his Papa, Mama, two brothers, and two sisters who were all waiting for his decision. Naughty Nello put down his fork and made his announcement, "Papa and Mama, you were right. The Old Sausage is best!"

Papa and Mama just laughed. Then everyone laughed even Naughty Nello.

Naughty Nello meant to keep his promise to be a very good boy and not get into any more trouble. However, Naughty Nello was still curious and some times he forgot to think before he did some things. There were still many lessons for him to learn.